Ginger Green

The New Friend

by Kim Kane
illustrated by Jon Davis

Curious Fox
a capstone company-publishers for children

*For my dear friend Jane C-R and
her lovely Skye. And for Martha,
my 3-foot muse, to whom Ginger
owes every ounce of her vim.*

– Kim

First published in 2018 by Curious Fox, an imprint of Capstone Global
Library Limited, 264 Banbury Road, Oxford, OX2 7DY – Registered
company number: 6695582
www.curious-fox.com

The author's moral rights are hereby asserted.

ISBN 978 1 78202 782 9
21 20 19 18 17
10 9 8 7 6 5 4 3 2 1

A CIP catalogue for this book is available from the British Library.

Ginger Green, Playdate Queen – *The New Friend*
Text Copyright © 2016 Kim Kane
Illustration Copyright © 2016 Jon Davis
Series Design Copyright © 2016 Hardie Grant Egmont
First published in Australia by Hardie Grant Egmont 2016

Printed and bound in India.

Contents

Chapter
One

My name is Ginger Green.

I am seven years old.

I am the Playdate Queen!

This afternoon, my friend Skye
is coming over.

Skye is my new friend from ballet. Skye has never been to my house.

Skye does not know that my house is tall like a tree house.

Skye does not know that
my bed is tall like a stage.

Last Saturday at ballet, I said,
"Skye, I am Ginger Green,
Playdate Queen. Would you like
to come and play with me?"

Skye turned

pink.

After class, Skye's dad said,

"YES!"

At twelve o'clock, the
doorbell rings.

DING
DONG!

It is Skye and her dad.

Mum says,

"Come in!"

Skye comes in.

Skye's dad comes in too.

"I'll wait until the girls are settled," says Skye's dad.

"Of course," says Mum.

She smiles, but I can see
that Mum is not happy.

Saturday is for making beds.

Saturday is for reading the paper.

Mum does not want to make coffee for Skye's dad.

"What do you want to play?"
I ask Skye.

I don't know what my new
friend Skye likes to do.

Skye turns pink.

Skye says nothing. She looks at her boots.

"Skye likes to play dressing-up," says Skye's dad.

"Great," I say. "I am Ginger Green, Playdate Queen!

I LOVE
dressing up."

I open the dressing-up box.

Skye takes a pointy hat
and a wand.

"I am a

witch," she says.

Skye's dad laughs.

I put on a pirate hat and a swishy skirt. I grab a parrot and a sword.

"I am Ginger Green, Pirate Queen!" I yell.

"**Arrrrr,** me hearties," says Skye's dad.

I stop. I feel my cheeks turn **pink**.

"Don't mind me," says Skye's dad.

Skye's dad is kind, but it's hard
to play dressing-up with a dad
in the room.

I do not feel like a Pirate Queen anymore. I **cannot** find my pirate voice.

Chapter Two

Mum hands Skye's dad a cup of coffee. He says thanks.

"Let's go to my room," I say.

We go to my bedroom.

It is actually **our** bedroom. I share it with my big sister, Violet.

Violet is reading on the bed.
Violet likes to read.

"Hi," says Skye's dad.

"Hi," says Violet.

She has to.

Violet can ignore me. And Violet does ignore me.

But Violet cannot ignore a grown-up.

Violet looks at me.

Her eyebrows are

SCRUNCHED.

I can tell Violet thinks it is weird that Skye's dad is here.

I think it's weird Skye's dad is here.

"Should I go?" asks Skye's dad.

"Stay," says Skye.

Skye does not think it is weird.

I sit on the floor near my dollhouse.

Skye sits on the floor.

Skye's dad sits on the floor too.

His knees come up past his chin.

I try to **ignore** Skye's dad.

I try to **ignore** his knees.

I pick up the dolls.

"Do you want to be the mum or the dad?"

I ask Skye.

"The mum," says Skye.

"The mum please," says
Skye's dad.

I pick up the baby.

I pick up the big sister.

But I am **NOT** in the mood.

It is hard to play with Violet
in the room.

It is harder to play with Skye's dad in the room.

I cannot find the voices.

I put the dolls down.

Skye is my new friend.

New friends are tricky.

I do not know
what new
friends like.

I look around.

I see Skye's ballet tights.

I see my tights.

I do know Skye LOVES dancing.

I LOVE dancing.

We both LOVE dancing.

We must dance!

Chapter Three

I get up. "Let's dance," I say.
"We can have a dance party!"

Skye smiles.

Violet gets up.
"It is too **hard** to read in here," she says. "I am going to the kitchen."

Skye looks at her dad.

Skye's dad looks at Skye.

I turn on some music.

I turn it up LOUD.

It is fun music.

It makes me want to JUMP.

It makes me want to KICK.

It makes me want to
WAVE my arms.

I am Ginger Green,

DISCO QUEEN!

I love to dance.

Skye stands up.

Skye JUMPS to the music.

Skye KICKS to the music.

Skye WAVES her
arms to the music.

Skye's dad stands up.

He JUMPS to the music.

He does BIG jumps

with his

BIG

knees.

I am Ginger Green, Disco
Queen, but it is too **hard**
to dance with Skye's dad
in the room.

I stop. Skye stops too.

Skye rolls her eyes.

"You can go now, Dad," says Skye.

"Are you sure?" asks Skye's dad.

Skye gives him a little push.

"It is **hard** to dance with a dad in the room," she says.

Skye's dad gives her a kiss.

"I am a **good** dancer," he says.

"Very good," says Skye. "But Ginger Green is the Disco Queen."

"Skye is a disco queen too!"

I shout.

I JUMP

up on my bed.

It is tall like a stage.

My new friend Skye takes off her boots and JUMPS up on the bed too.

She smiles.

Her smile is big and happy.

Her smile is as happy as the music.

"I'll be back at three o'clock,"
says Skye's dad.

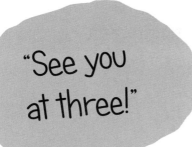

"See you at three!"

Skye shouts.

"See you at three!" I shout.

Then we **turn up**
the music even louder.

We **KICK**
even higher.

We **JUMP**
even higher too.

My new friend Skye is sometimes
a bit shy.

My new friend Skye is sometimes
a bit scared.

But my new friend
Skye LOVES to dance.

I am Ginger Green, Playdate Queen, and I LOVE playdates.

Playdates with new friends are
a bit like a PUZZLE.

Sometimes
it just takes
time to work
out what new
friends like.

My new friend Skye needs her
dad to start.

But my new friend Skye

LOVES

to dance.

My new friend Skye loves to dance with me.

THE END

About the
author

Kim Kane

Kim Kane is an award-winning author
who writes for children and teenagers
in Australia and overseas. Kim's books
include the CBCA short-listed picture
book *Family Forest* and her children's
novel *Pip: the Story of Olive*. Kim lives with
her family in Melbourne, Australia, and
writes whenever and wherever she can.

About the illustrator

Jon Davis

Pirates, old elephants, witches in bloomers, bears on bikes, ugly cats, sweet kids – Jon Davis does it all! Based in Twickenham, United Kingdom, Jon Davis has illustrated more than forty kids' books for publishers across the globe.

For more exciting books from
brilliant authors, follow the fox!

www.curious-fox.com